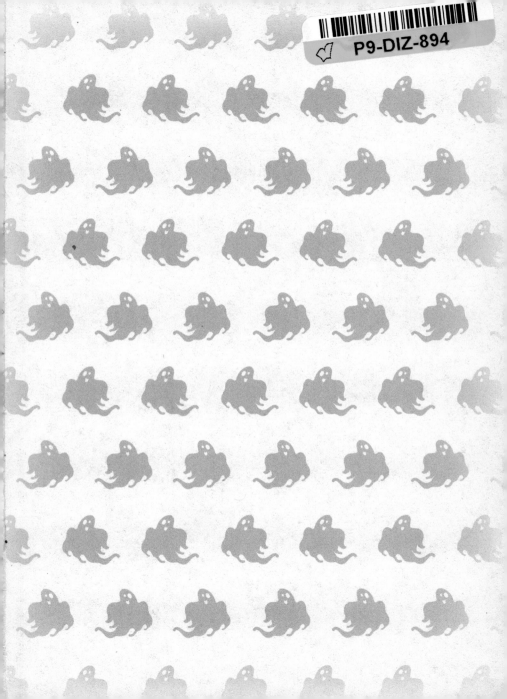

DESMOND COLE GHOST PATROL

ESCAPE FROM THE ROLLER GHOSTER

by **Andres Miedoso**

illustrated by **Victor Rivas**

with **Kirk Parrish**

LITTLE SIMON

New York London Toronto Sydney New Delhi

This book is a work of fiction. Any references to historical events, real people, or real places are used fictitiously. Other names, characters, places, and events are products of the author's imagination, and any resemblance to actual events or places or persons, living or dead, is entirely coincidental.

LITTLE SIMON

An imprint of Simon & Schuster Children's Publishing Division
1230 Avenue of the Americas, New York, New York 10020
First Little Simon paperback edition July 2020
Copyright © 2020 by Simon & Schuster, Inc.
Also available in a Little Simon hardcover edition.
All rights reserved, including the right of reproduction in whole or in part in any form.
LITTLE SIMON is a registered trademark of Simon & Schuster, Inc.,
and associated colophon is a trademark of Simon & Schuster, Inc.
For information about special discounts for bulk purchases, please contact
Simon & Schuster Special Sales at 1-866-506-1949 or business@simonandschuster.com.
The Simon & Schuster Speakers Bureau can bring authors to your live event. For more information
or to book an event contact the Simon & Schuster Speakers Bureau at 1-866-248-3049
or visit our website at www.simonspeakers.com.
Designed by Steve Scott
Manufactured in the United States of America 0220 BVG
4 6 8 10 9 7 5 3
Library of Congress Cataloging-in-Publication Data
Names: Miedoso, Andres, author. | Rivas, Victor, illustrator.
Title: Escape from the Roller Ghoster / by Andres Miedoso ; illustrated by Victor Rivas.
Description: First Little Simon paperback edition. | New York : Little Simon, 2020.
Series: Desmond Cole ghost patrol ; 11 | Audience: Ages 5–9. | Audience: Grades K–1.
Summary: Desmond and Andres try to enjoy their day at the local theme park
while being pursued by ghosts.
Identifiers: LCCN 2019055176 | ISBN 9781534464902 (paperback) |
ISBN 9781534464919 (hardcover) | ISBN 9781534464926 (eBook)
Subjects: CYAC: Amusement parks—Fiction. | Ghosts—Fiction. |
Friendship—Fiction. | African Americans—Fiction. | Hispanic Americans—Fiction.
Classification: LCC PZ7.1.M518 Es 2020 | DDC [Fic]—dc23
LC record available at https://lccn.loc.gov/2019055176

CONTENTS

CHAPTER ONE

BIZARRO ZONE

When it comes to weird towns, no one beats Kersville. Seriously! We've got it all here.

Ghosts riding bikes? Check.

Dancing ghouls? Check.

Sleepwalking snowmen? Check.

Werewolves? Not yet.

Of course, there's one weird part of this town that's the best kind of weird. It's the wildest place in the world. Yes, Kersville has its very own theme park—Bizarro Zone!

Bizarro Zone has tons of rides—right-side-up rides, upside-down rides, swingy rides, and splashy rides!

If you don't like rides, then Bizarro Zone has games! They have video games and win-a-prize games that have the *best* prizes. One time I won a stuffed lobster that was so big that my dad had to tie it to the roof of the car!

And if you don't like rides or games or prizes, then WHAT *DO* YOU LIKE?

I'm kidding. If you don't like that stuff, Bizarro Zone still has you covered. Because no matter what you *don't* like, *everybody* likes food.

Well, the food at Bizarro Zone is yummy and *HUGE*! Their burritos are so big that you need help eating them. Their pizza slices are the largest you've ever seen. One day this kid was trying to eat hers, and a gust of wind carried her away like a kite!

But there's one thing Bizarro Zone is *famous* for: the Bizarro Biggie Sundae. It has thirty scoops of ice cream topped with chocolate chunks, caramel sauce, bananas, and whipped cream. Even the spoons are made of fried dough.

No one has ever finished the Bizarro Biggie Sundae—not even close!

That could change today because my best friend, Desmond Cole, has his mind set on eating that sundae.

But first, we needed to try Bizarro Zone's newest ride. It's called the Roller Ghoster.

Yeah, that's me, Andres Miedoso. I'm the one with my hands in the air, screaming my head off. That's how scary this ride is.

Desmond is right next to me. His hands are in the air too, but he's not scared. He's excited. That's because we are the Ghost Patrol, and we have a new case to solve.

You see, Bizarro Zone is just like a lot of other places in Kersville.

It's haunted.

DESMOND COLE

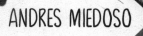

ANDRES MIEDOSO

CHAPTER TWO

THE LONGEST LINE

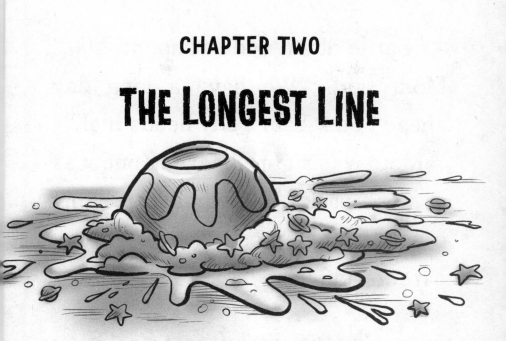

You know what they say: Never start a ghost story with a ghost. So, let's start from this morning.

My parents were taking me to Bizarro Zone. I was *way* past excited, so I couldn't sit still at the kitchen table, and things got a little messy.

"Settle down and eat up, *mi hijo*," Mom said. "We have a long day ahead of us. Your body needs fuel."

Mom was right. Bizarro Zone was a *huge* park. We would probably break the step-count app on my parents' phones!

I was about to take a calm bite when the doorbell rang. It was Desmond. He was coming with us to Bizarro Zone.

Dad pulled out a chair for Desmond and invited him to have breakfast with us.

"No, thanks, Mr. Miedoso," said Desmond.

My brain couldn't believe my ears. Desmond *never* turned down food unless it was made by his own parents. They were *not* good cooks.

Was I dreaming? I pinched myself and *ouch*! This was very real.

"Are you feeling okay?" I asked, checking Desmond the way my mom does when I'm sick.

"Yeah," Desmond said with an excited grin.

"I'm saving room for Bizarro Zone. This is the year, Andres!"

"The year for what?" I asked.

"This is the year I'm going to finish the Bizarro Biggie Sundae," Desmond replied.

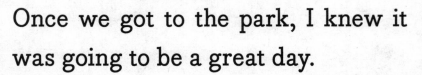

Once we got to the park, I knew it was going to be a great day.

The sun was out, but it wasn't too hot. Just when you started to sweat, there was a nice, refreshing breeze.

It was perfect until we got to the entrance.

We were the last ones in the longest line I had ever seen. It looked like everybody in the whole *world* was there!

"We're going to be waiting all day!" I cried.

But Desmond stayed calm, as

always. He pulled out a map of the amusement park and said, "Let's plan our day while we wait."

The line moved like a lazy snail, and we were able to plan everything—every single ride and all our games. There was only one thing we didn't plan for . . . dumb luck.

CHAPTER THREE

STEP RIGHT UP

"Excuse me. Are you Desmond Cole?"

A teenage park worker in a sloppy uniform stood beside us. He looked worried.

Maybe that's because my parents started grilling him with a million parent-type questions.

"Who is asking for Desmond?"

"What do they want with him?"

"Does your mother know you're walking around without your shirt tucked in?"

Now the worker looked terrified.

"P-please don't tell my mother about my shirt," he begged. "And, uh, my boss asked me to find Desmond Cole and give him this."

The worker held out a box filled with four bracelets.

I swear that I heard angels singing as the sun shined directly on that box.

It was amazing!

They weren't just bracelets. Nope, they were VIP passes. "VIP" means "Very Important Person."

Anyone wearing those bracelets got to skip all the lines and go straight onto the rides. Not only that—VIPs got free food and played free games!

I thought only famous people got these, but now . . . WE WERE VIPS TOO!

Desmond was frozen. He just stared at the box with his mouth hanging open.

So I told the park worker, "Yes, he's Desmond Cole, and yes, we'll take those VIP passes!"

Then, before I could take the box, Desmond said, "Hold on, mystery dude. Why is your boss giving me VIP passes?"

The teenager shrugged and said, "How should I know? I just work here. Do you want the passes or not?"

Desmond took a moment to think. It was only for a few seconds, but they were the longest seconds of my life.

Finally, he smiled and said, "Sure, we'll take them. Thanks."

As we put on the bracelets, we heard a loud **BOOM**. It sounded like a clap of thunder, but there wasn't a storm cloud in sight.

"What was that?" I shrieked.

"Oh, that's our new ride, the Roller Ghoster," the worker said with a shudder. "It's too creepy for me."

I looked up at the rides towering behind the entrance, and there it was: the Roller Ghoster. It was huge, with a mega-steep drop, plus loop-the-loops, corkscrews, and enough twists and turns to make anyone lose their lunch.

Who would want to ride a roller coaster like that?

The park worker took us straight to the front of the line. The other people in the crowd gasped when they noticed our VIP bracelets.

I felt so special!

The worker scanned our bracelets, opened the front gates, and said, "Step right up. Welcome to Bizarro Zone."

CHAPTER FOUR

TILT-A-HURL

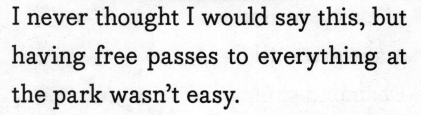

I never thought I would say this, but having free passes to everything at the park wasn't easy.

There was so much we could do that it was hard to figure out what to do first.

The rides around us were huge!

"Let's play games," I suggested.

Desmond shook his head. "Just because the games are free, it doesn't mean we're going to win them. And losing a game is a bad way to start the day."

"But what if we win?" I asked.

"Then we'd have to carry around a giant prize all day," Desmond said. "No, thanks."

He was right. That would not be cool.

Then the yummy smells from the food stands drifted through the air. "We could eat!" I said.

Desmond patted his belly. "Sorry, Andres. I'm saving room for the Bizarro Biggie Sundae."

Having fun was suddenly harder than I thought.

"Here's an idea," said Desmond. "Let's go on the Roller Ghoster!"

When I heard him say "Roller Ghoster," I did what any kid would do.

I cried.

Okay, I didn't *baby* cry. But one tear *did* roll down my cheek.

"Uh, um," I whimpered. "Why don't we start with one of the, um, *easier* rides?"

Desmond nodded. "Good idea. Let's work our way up to the Roller Ghoster!"

Phew. I could breathe again.

"How about the Tilt-A-Hurl?" Desmond suggested.

I had never been on that ride before, but it didn't look too scary. It was a bunch of colorful pods that spun around in circles. How bad could it be?

TILT-A-HURL

We walked to the front of the long line and had our bracelets scanned. Then Desmond and I climbed into one pod while my parents rode in the pod next to us.

"Don't look so worried, Andres," Mom said. "It's going to be fine."

"That's easy for you to say," I mumbled under my breath. My parents loved swirly-twirly rides.

CLANG!

The safety bar banged into place. I couldn't change my mind anymore. I was locked in.

The ride started, and right away, Desmond smashed into me as we spun around and around.

Then we started to tilt a little. Then we started to tilt *a lot*! Before I knew it, we weren't sitting anymore. We were stuck to the wall of the pod!

That was when I did something I never thought I would do on a ride like this.

I smiled. I smiled *big*.

So did Desmond. And we both screamed as the wind hit our faces and stretched them out in every silly direction.

We looked hilarious!

I looked over to my parents, but their pod looked different from ours. It was glowing! And it had a face.

A *ghost* face.

A ghost face that winked.

Their pod spun faster and faster until it was nothing more than a blur. Then the ghost stretched over to Desmond and me.

"Are you having fun yet?" it asked in the spookiest voice ever.

Then it disappeared.

Yep. A *ghost* just asked us if we were having fun.

If anyone else had asked me that question, I would have said, "Yes, I'm having a great time."

But now, I wasn't so sure.

CHAPTER FIVE

SCARY-GO-ROUND

After the ride ended, Desmond and I ran over to my parents. They were looking kind of . . . green.

"Mom and Dad," I said, "are you okay?"

"Sure," Mom replied, walking with shaky legs. "We're just a little dizzy."

Then my dad asked, "Can someone make the world stop turning?"

"But, Dad," I said, "isn't the world supposed to turn?"

"Not *this* fast!" he responded.

We helped my parents wobble over to a bench.

"Boys, the amusement park isn't so amusing to us right now," Mom said. "You go ahead, and we'll catch up with you later."

Dad cupped his hands over his mouth and his eyes got really big. "Ugh, don't say 'ketchup.'"

Oh no. I knew that look. We need to escape before Dad hurled.

"Thanks, Mom!" was all I said, and Desmond and I took off running. I mean, we were VIPs. We still had a whole day of fun left, and that would end fast if my parents got sick!

"What's up next?" I asked.

"The Scary-Go-Round," Desmond replied.

The Scary-Go-Round was just a merry-go-round with zombie zoo animals. There was nothing scary about that ride. Even the zombie animals looked cute.

Suddenly I saw that Desmond was searching for something.

"Desmond," I whispered. "Is it Ghost Patrol time?"

"Did you see what happened on the last ride?" he asked.

I nodded. How could I *not* see something that creepy?

Desmond continued. "That ghost was trying to get our attention. It might try to reach us again on another ride."

We walked to the front of the long line and had our bracelets scanned. Then we climbed onto the Scary-Go-Round.

Desmond hopped on a zombie pig, and I got on a zombie ostrich. When the ride started, I braced for something weird to happen. Would the zombie animals come to life and say, "Give us brains"?

Instead, the ride spun slowly. It was so slow that parents standing next to their kids didn't even need to hold on. Everything was fine.

Then the music started, and boy, was it super-eerie!

All the instruments were out of tune. It sounded like a band of gremlins who didn't know how to play!

As the melody echoed off-key, a mist gathered around us. If you find yourself surrounded by mist and creepy music, it's never a good sign.

And just like that, we found our ghost . . . or the ghost found us.

CHAPTER SIX

KIDDIE RIDES

Here's a good way to ruin a perfectly fun day: Have a ghost show up and scare you!

"Desmond Cole," the ghost said in a deep groan.

It didn't sound like a regular ghost. Trust me, I know.

Ever since I moved to Kersville, I've met more than my fair share of ghosts!

This ghost was different. It sounded like pretend ghosts that you see on TV or in the movies. Those ghosts were always whispering or moaning. They acted like talking was the hardest thing to do in the world.

In real life, ghosts sound just like living people.

"Follow me," the ghost moaned in that spooky voice. The ride stopped, and the ghost floated away.

I knew what would happen next: Desmond was going to follow the ghost.

So I followed Desmond.

The ghost led us through the kiddie park area, where they had the small, boring baby rides.

"Get on the Puffy Pony Train," the ghost whispered.

The Puffy Pony Train was just a bunch of pony cars on a round track.

The only fun thing about it was the cotton candy tree that had a tunnel for the train to go through.

Desmond and I walked to the front of another superlong line.

Being VIPs was really the best.

Once we were on the train, the ghost sat in the engine car and acted like our conductor.

"All aboard for the Puffy Pony adventure!" said the ghost. "Please buckle up and keep your hands inside the Puffy Pony car at all times."

TOOT-TOOT!

Puffs of glitter rose in the air, and the train started moving . . . just as slowly as the Scary-Go-Round.

The little kids waiting in line waved to us as we went by. I started to wave back, but the ghost screamed, "Keep your hands inside the car!"

"Sorry!" I said. "I was just trying to be nice!"

The train rounded the circle, and finally we entered the cotton candy tree tunnel.

Once we were inside, the strangest thing happened. Our seats opened up from under us, and Desmond and I tumbled down a long slide that led to an underground room filled with large TV screens.

"What in the world is—" I stopped my question right in the middle as an old man in a chair turned around to face us.

"Welcome to the Bizarro Zone control center," he said. "I'm Mr. Bizarro, and I've brought you here because I need your help."

CHAPTER SEVEN

THE ROLLER GHOSTER

Desmond and I were standing in front of the one and only Mr. Bizarro, the creator of Bizarro Zone!

Inside, I was freaking out. But Desmond was completely cool.

"I knew your ghost wasn't real," he told Mr. Bizarro.

"I needed to get your attention," Mr. Bizarro declared. "That ghost was a leftover hologram from our Halloween show last year. I beamed it down from the projectors set up around the park to lead you here."

"That was very clever," Desmond said. He almost looked like he was impressed.

But *I* wasn't.

"Why did you have to make my parents so dizzy?" I asked him.

Mr. Bizarro turned to me and said, "I'm sorry about that, but your parents might not understand why we need the Ghost Patrol. You see, Bizarro Zone is haunted."

"Yeah, haunted with fake ghosts," said Desmond.

"Oh, we have real ghosts too," explained Mr. Bizarro. "And they are causing real problems at the park."

"Huh. We didn't notice anything wrong," I told him. "I mean, except for the long lines. If we didn't have VIP passes, we'd still be waiting to get into the park!"

"That's the biggest problem," Mr. Bizarro said with a sigh. "Ever since our Roller Ghoster ride launched, the lines have been much too crowded. We thought more people were coming to the park, but that's not the case. Take a look at this."

Mr. Bizarro pointed to the wall of monitors behind him. They showed videos of different rides from around the park that seemed normal. But when we looked closer, we saw that the rides had lots of empty seats.

"It's not just people coming to the park," Desmond whispered, pulling out a weird pair of glasses from his pocket. He put them on, looked at the screens again, and nodded.

I nodded too, even though I had absolutely no idea why. Well, until Desmond handed me his glasses. That was when everything changed.

Suddenly, all I could see were ghosts! They were everywhere.

They were playing games, eating food, and riding rides! But what really made me mad was how they were cutting the lines.

AND THEY DIDN'T EVEN HAVE VIP PASSES!

"Hey, that's not cool," I said. "We can't let those ghosts get away with this!"

"I need your help, Desmond," said Mr. Bizarro. "If these ghosts keep making human visitors wait in line, then people are going to stop coming. I'll have to shut Bizarro Zone down."

"Well, we can't let that happen," Desmond said. "I have a plan."

Of course he did!

CHAPTER EIGHT

We Have a Winner

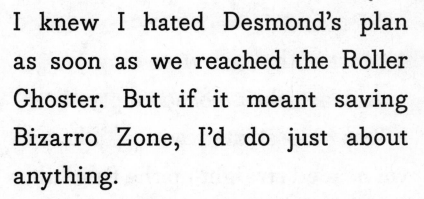

I knew I hated Desmond's plan as soon as we reached the Roller Ghoster. But if it meant saving Bizarro Zone, I'd do just about anything.

We charged to the front of the line and flashed our VIP bracelets.

Most of the cars were empty.

At least, they *looked* empty.

The ride started with a jolt, and we headed straight up the first hill.

Without warning, Desmond made an announcement.

"Okay, fellow riders. We know you're here, so show yourselves."

The ghosts appeared right in front of our eyes. They were in every single seat—talk about a Roller *Ghoster*!

Then Desmond took his plan to the next level by saying, "I challenge all of you to a Bizarro contest. The winners get the amusement park. The losers leave forever. Do you accept?"

The ghosts nodded.

"Okay," said Desmond. "The first challenge is to ride the entire Roller Ghoster with your hands in the air starting now!"

Desmond and I raised our hands and got ready to scream. No matter how twisty the loops or how steep the drops, we had to keep our hands high in the air. And you know what? After I stopped being scared, the ride was really, *really* fun!

The ghosts, on the other hand, were all fraidy-cats. They had to hold on tight.

When the ride stopped, Desmond and I realized we had won!

Now all we had to do was keep on winning, because next up were the park games.

"Okay," Desmond told the crowd of ghosts, "whoever has the most stuffed animals at the end of this challenge wins!"

And it was on!

We played the Fishbowl Toss first. Desmond was the only one to get a Ping-Pong ball into the fishbowl. He won a giant stuffed goldfish.

Then we played the Hotshot basketball game, but it wasn't very fair. The ghost next to me had arms so long that all it had to do was reach out and drop the ball into the basket.

The ghost won easily and got a stuffed candy cane.

"Don't worry about it," Desmond told me. "We have a lot more games to play."

The Water Blaster Blast Off was next. I've always loved this game. I got in position, and a few seconds later, we heard "Ready, set, blast!"

I aimed my water blaster straight
at the alien's mouth and watched as
my rocket ship climbed higher and
higher. The first one to reach Mars
would win. And guess what? I won!
Plus, I got a huge stuffed alien.

The next game was Bottle Crash. The first person or ghost to knock down the stack of bottles with a baseball would win. Desmond threw a pitch and barely missed the bottles.

Then it was the ghost's turn. Apparently, things aren't exactly fair when you play against ghosts.

Instead of using the baseball, the sneaky ghost shot a fireball that hit the stack of bottles and turned them all to ash!

"That's against the rules!" I cried. But it didn't matter. The ghost took its adorable stuffed teddy bear and gave it a big hug.

This went on for a while because there were so many games at Bizarro Zone. When we reached the last game, the score was tied.

Desmond stepped up to the Test Your Strength stage. For this game, each player took a turn hitting a target with a hammer to make a heavy puck go up a high tower. The highest anyone could reach was 100. If you hit it, a bell rang. But nobody ever rang the bell. It's impossible. The bell at the top of the tower looked like it had never been touched.

Desmond flexed his muscles, picked up the hammer, and slammed it down. The metal puck climbed to 60!

I jumped and cheered until a giant ghost stepped out from the crowd.

It grabbed the hammer, which looked tiny in the ghost's hands. Then the ghost pounded the target, and the puck shot all the way up to 99.

Whoa.

The strong ghost handed me the hammer. "Your turn, human," it said with a smile.

It was up to me. Either I reached 100 on the Test Your Strength game, or kids would have to say good-bye to Bizarro Zone forever.

"This is for kids everywhere!" I screamed, feeling a surge of strength in my body.

Then I slammed the hammer down so hard that I flew right out of my shoes!

The puck raced up the tower in a blur. I had no idea how high it had gone until we heard the bell at the top clang loudly.

I couldn't believe it. I hit 100! And I won a huge unicorn.

Desmond tackled me into a pile of our stuffed animals, and all we could do was laugh. The ghosts had to leave Bizarro Zone forever, and there would never be long lines at our theme park again!

But when the ghosts surrounded us, we made a new discovery: Ghosts are sore losers!

CHAPTER NINE

TUNNEL OF LOVE

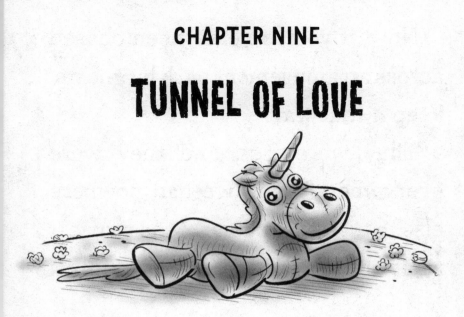

All those ghosts looked mad.

"H-here," I said, trying to give away one of my stuffed animals. But they didn't want it. They wanted *us*!

We did what anyone would do in that situation. We ran! And they chased us.

Now, if you've never been chased across an amusement park by ghosts, keep it that way!

They were fast, and they were everywhere! Soon we had nowhere else to turn except one of the scariest rides at the park: the Tunnel of Love.

Okay, it's not a scary ride. It's a *gross* ride unless you like all that lovey-dovey stuff.

Yuck!

Our only hope was that ghosts felt the same way about the ride as we did. This was the last place I would ever look for myself, believe me!

Desmond and I ran to the front of the line. The same teenager who'd brought us the VIP bracelets was working.

"Sorry, guys," he said. "This ride is for grown-ups only."

"But we are VIPs," Desmond reminded him as we jumped into a heart-shaped boat.

"And we're being chased by ghosts!" I added.

Before he could stop us, the boat pulled away.

Desmond and I were taken to a dark room filled with baby angels, birds chirping, and hearts decorating everything. Yes, it was yucky, but it was also safe.

Then we saw other couples holding hands in their boats.

Suddenly the Tunnel of Love became the Tunnel of *Blech*!

We needed to get out of there fast! Desmond spotted an exit, and we made a run for it.

The door creaked open, but the coast was clear.

That was when I felt a hand on my shoulder.

But it wasn't a ghost. It was the teenage park worker.

"That's it," he said angrily. "The two of you are banned from Bizarro Zone. *Forever!*"

"What!" I cried. "You can't do that!"

"We're VIPs," Desmond added.

The park worker just shook his head. "That doesn't mean you can break the rules," he said. "It's not fair to everyone else."

Just then the ghosts floated in
and said, "That's right! These tiny
humans have to follow the rules."

Well, when the park worker saw
the ghosts, he ran away screaming.

I didn't feel like running anymore. Actually, I felt kind of sad and mad at the same time. We were banned from the world's best amusement park . . . just like we banned the ghosts.

Desmond looked like he felt the same way. "Andres, you know how we're feeling right now? Well, that's probably how the ghosts feel."

"But they broke the rules," I said. "They were cutting the lines."

"We broke the rules too," Desmond said.

He was right. It wasn't fair to kick the ghosts out. But what could we do?

Then Desmond got a look in his eyes and turned to face the glowing crowd. "Ghost friends, I have a plan that will make everyone happy."

CHAPTER TEN

SCREAM FOR ICE CREAM!

Desmond's idea was simple. Bizarro Zone would stay open late just for the ghosts! After all, people need to sleep at night, but ghosts can visit the park whenever!

So when the human crowds leave, the ghost crowds can come in!

We went on opening night, and it was amazing. Now that people aren't there, the ghosts don't have to be invisible anymore. And let me tell you that they had the time of their lives!

Mr. Bizarro even allows the ghosts
to sleep in the haunted house all day
if they want.

POPCORN

Of course, they sometimes wake up early and scare the riders, but that's what you get when you go on the haunted house ride. I mean, you can never have too many ghosts in there!

And guess what? Desmond's idea worked. The lines at Bizarro Zone are much shorter, and people can

ride a lot more rides. Who knew that a day at Bizarro Zone could be even more fun than it was before?!

Oh, and Mr. Bizarro was so happy with how everything turned out that he said we could come back whenever we wanted. He even let us keep our VIP bracelets!

I know, I know. You're wondering if Desmond ever got the chance to eat the Bizarro Biggie Sundae. Well, he did.

And you know what? He totally finished the whole thing!